FEATHERS

For Jacinta xxx — P.C.

To Eunice Andrada, for making me feel safe and warm.
And to Reuben, who has a smile bright enough to read good books by — P.L.

Scholastic Canada Ltd.
604 King Street West, Toronto, Ontario M5V 1E1, Canada

Scholastic Inc.
557 Broadway, New York, NY 10012, USA

Scholastic Australia Pty Limited
PO Box 579, Gosford, NSW 2250, Australia

Scholastic New Zealand Limited
Private Bag 94407, Botany, Manukau 2163, New Zealand

Scholastic Children's Books
Euston House, 24 Eversholt Street, London NW1 1DB, UK

www.scholastic.ca

Library and Archives Canada Cataloguing in Publication

Cummings, Phil, author
Feathers / by Phil Cummings ; illustrated by Phil Lesnie.

Previously published: Lindfield, N.S.W.: Scholastic Australia, 2017.
ISBN 978-1-4431-2887-2 (hardcover)

I. Lesnie, Phil, 1985-, illustrator II. Title.
PZ7.C97Fe 2018   j823'.914   C2017-904986-0

First published by Scholastic Australia in 2017.
This edition published by Scholastic Canada Ltd. in 2018.

6 5 4 3 2 1   Printed in China 127   17 18 19 20 21

FEATHERS

Phil Cummings & Phil Lesnie

Scholastic Canada Ltd.
Toronto New York London Auckland Sydney
Mexico City New Delhi Hong Kong Buenos Aires

The sun rose on a crisp, cloudy day.

The sandpiper stretched its wings
in the chilling breeze.

It knew it was time to leave

so it took flight.

It soared through whirlwinds of tumbling leaves
that fluttered

like butterflies.

On . . .

    and on . . .

        and on it flew,

across borders only seen on maps.

It flew over a crumbled village where a small boy sheltered,
hoping the earth would never quake again.
The sandpiper's shadow swept across the rubble
of the boy's once-safe home.

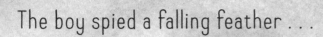

The boy spied a falling feather . . .

spinning

and drifting.

He climbed to the top of a craggy mountain and caught it.

It was soft and smooth on his grimy cheek.

The bird continued on its way.

It flew over snow-capped mountains

and deep river valleys.

It flew through long nights

where the spit of gunfire

bit into the darkness.

When morning came
it flew low over fleeing families

walking in lines like ants.

A girl at the end of the line had her world bundled on her back.

She saw a fallen feather at her feet.
She picked it up and tickled her brother's toes.
The echo of their laughter

        drifted away

               with the dust.

The bird left the laughter behind.

There was still such a long way to go.

It headed into a dark storm

of deafening thunder,

wild wind

and rain.

When the storm passed,
the bird emerged from shredding clouds,

drifting apart

like pieces

of a broken puzzle.

The land below was flooded.

The houses were islands in a sea of brown.

The sun broke through the clouds and shone on a fragile feather
floating in the water.

A mother reached out. She took the feather in her gentle fingers, dried it and made a boat for her children.

They placed their boat on the water and dreamed of sailing away.

The bird headed away from the brown floodwaters and out over blue oceans.
Waves rose like mountains.

The bird was tired but it knew it was getting
closer to where it would be safe and warm.

It swooped down to the shimmering water near Mia's house, calm and quiet.

Mia saw it coming.
As it glided in, she spied a falling feather,

spinning and drifting.

Mia ran and caught it
before it hit the ground.

She looked at the feather.

She liked the way it caught the light;
the colours, the smoothness

. . . perfect.

"Dad," she said. "Look what I caught!"

"Wow!" said Dad. "Aren't you lucky?"

Mia smiled. "Yes, I am," she said.

Not far from Mia's house, the bird
rested at the water's edge . . .

safe and warm.